THE GLASS ANGELS

SUSAN HILL

illustrated by Valerie Littlewood

CANDLEWICK PRESS
CAMBRIDGE, MASSACHUSETTS

CHAPTER

1

"Wait," said Tilly, "wait. You're walking too fast."

But just as she spoke they came around the corner and out of the shelter of houses onto the sea front, and her voice was caught up on the whirl of the wind and drowned in the boom of the sea below. So her mother didn't hear her.

It was raining too, hard, cold rain like pins on their faces. For once, Tilly was quite glad that her raincoat had been somebody else's and so was too big. It came right down her legs, to meet and overlap the top of her boots, and below the tips of her fingers and almost up to her ears. Only her face and the front of her hair were getting really wet.

She stumbled, trying to keep up, and then at last her mother slowed down and shifted her bag, which was full of the pins and measuring tape, the patterns and fabric scraps and chalk, onto the other arm, so she could take hold of Tilly's hand and as she did so, she squeezed it briefly. It was a squeeze that meant a lot of things, Tilly knew. It meant understanding and friendliness and sharing Tilly's feelings about the walk home in the dark and cold and rain; it meant thank you to Tilly for sitting so long by herself on the tight-buttoned chair in Miss Kendall's back parlor and not interrupting at all while Miss Kendall was being measured and fitted and made a fuss of; it meant everything's all right and we're going home now, it's not too far and we've got one another.

So Tilly squeezed back and her squeeze meant a lot of the same things, and a few others of her own besides.

Anyway, she hadn't really minded sitting in Miss Kendall's parlor, though there had been nothing to do there except look at the row of encyclopedias, and piles of old yellow magazines about India and Africa, which were full of pictures that Tilly found either very dull or very frightening.

They had made up a fire for her and brought her a glass of milk and a fat square of gingerbread, and she had gone off into a peaceful, dreamy state, like a bird hovering on the air, not thinking, not sleeping, just breathing softly, just *being*.

The parlor was a sad room, as if no one ever went in there to talk and laugh and leave things lying around. There was a bloom of dust lying over the polish of the table, and none of the furniture quite matched, and the pictures on the walls were the kind no one ever wanted to look at, but all the same couldn't quite be bothered to get rid of.

Still, she was very used to it, visiting other people's houses with her mother, and having to sit quietly in a

corner somewhere and not be a nuisance while the customer had a fitting. Very occasionally, one of them came to the apartment. But Tilly knew her mother didn't encourage that.

"My home is my home," she said.

But Tilly thought that was not the only reason. There was so little room, and most of that was full of the sewing table and the treadle machine, the tailor's dummy and the parcels of cloth, and the rail on which the half-made-up garments hung.

"People like me to fit them in their own homes, in comfort, and at their convenience," Tilly's mother said.

Which was why they were stomping home through all the wind and wet and dark of an evening two weeks before Christmas.

Christmas! As the word dropped down like a penny into the slot of her mind, Tilly slackened her steps, feeling a spurt of excitement. Perhaps, thanks to Miss Kendall, there might be something special about Christmas this year.

In the spring, Miss Kendall was to be married, and Tilly's mother was being employed to make the wedding dress and the bridesmaids' dresses, and all the clothes for Miss Kendall's going-away and her honeymoon, and that was a very good order indeed, one of the biggest her mother had ever had. It meant that there wouldn't have to be worry about the rent and the gas bill and the coal bill and the grocer's bill and Tilly's shoes, for some while. It might even mean there wouldn't be so much worry about Christmas.

But Tilly wouldn't mention that, she dared not, only hugged the thought inside her and felt a hope flickering like the coals of a small bright fire, that she would keep going herself in secret.

There was no one else walking along the esplanade. Only one or two of the street lamps were lit, and in between the pools of light those threw onto the pavement were yards and yards of darkness, like rivers they had to plunge into, Tilly thought, and cross as quickly as possible in order to reach the safety and brightness of the other side.

In the summer along here, fairy lights were strung from the trees like the colored glass beads of a necklace, and music and voices came out of the hotels and people strolled up and down enjoying the warm evening air. But no one came on a seaside holiday in December; the hotels and guest houses were closed and shuttered, though here and there, in between, was a tall house in which people lived, and a light shone from behind the curtains, making it seem more friendly.

They were walking close to the railings; once or twice Tilly put out her hand to brush against them and a chain of raindrops slid off onto her sleeve. On the other side of the railings, in the darkest of the darkness, lay the gardens, and the path that wound down and down to the seashore.

In summer there were miles of flat honey-colored sand in a curve around the bay, and the sea lay still and far out and deep blue; there were deck chairs and donkeys, buckets and spades and ice cream—and people, people, people.

How strange it is, thought Tilly, that in the middle of winter the summer seems like a dream, you can scarcely imagine it or believe it ever happened, and in the summer you sit on the hot sand in the sunshine and wonder how the winter cold and dark and emptiness could ever, ever, have been.

At the end of the esplanade, they turned and followed the curve of the road and then the sound of the sea faded, shut out by the tall houses. There were more lights in windows now, and a car went by, and a man was walking his dog; it began to feel less lonely. On the next corner, the sweet and tobacconist shop was still open and the sweet jars gleamed and glistened like jewels in the windows. There were paper chains draped between them.

Perhaps for Christmas...

Past the church. Another road, with front doors set back behind long thin paths, between privet hedges and laurel bushes. Five—seven—nine—home!

They had a privet hedge, too, high and straggling, and two stone pillars guarding the gate—but down the path it was dark.

Tilly looked up at the windows. There Mr. and Mrs. Day lived, then Miss Brookes, Mrs. Plant, the Babcocks, the people with the one-eyed cat. There was no window for themselves, their attic apartment looked over the back. But while her mother dug around in her purse for the front door key and the rain ran off her collar and down

her neck, Tilly was staring up at one particular window. The lamp was on and the shade of the lamp was a reddish color, so that its light glowed like the heart of a dark coal in the space where the curtains had been left slightly open. To Tilly, the light was more than a light, it was a message, a warmth, it beckoned her, it promised.

"Come inside child, do, no need to get more drenched than you already are. The clothes will take long enough to dry out as it is."

Her mother sounded suddenly weary. Tilly hopped quickly into the hall and the big door shut behind them, and they began the trudge up the five flights of stairs to the attic floor.

When they reached the second landing and saw the door at the end of the short passage, Tilly slowed her steps, wondering, wanting, but her mother frowned, glancing back over her shoulder, and shook her head, beckoning Tilly on.

Up another. The Babcocks. Then the people with the one-eyed cat.

And then the last, short, steep flight to their own attic rooms.

By the time they reached them, of course, the lights had gone out. They always did. You pressed the switch as you entered the downstairs hall, and then you had only so long to get all the way up to the top before it clicked off again, by itself. If she ran very fast, two stairs at a time, Tilly could *just* get to their door before the light went out but her mother climbed much more slowly, especially as she was almost always carrying something, shopping or washing, or just the sewing bag.

"Why can't there be lights that stay on until you don't need them anymore?"

"Because people would forget and leave them to burn and that would cost Mr. Simpkins money."

Mr. Simpkins, the hated landlord. All the inconveniences and discomforts of their life seemed to be the fault of Mr. Simpkins—leaky faucets, drafts, the hole in the floorboard under the sink, the window that rattled, the smell on the landing, the fact that you had to stand on a chair to read the gas meter, because Mr. Simpkins was too mean to get it moved.

And the lights that never stayed on long enough.

But an hour later, everything seemed all right again. The coats had been hung up to drip over the bathtub, and the meat-and-potato pie from yesterday had heated up nicely, with a can of peas, and then Tilly had had not one but two jam tarts, because her mother hadn't wanted to eat hers.

Now she sat on the rag rug beside the fire, drinking her cocoa and enjoying the pattering of the rain on the roof and the sputtering of the gas, and the *tok-tok-tok* of her mother's scissors across the cloth rolled out on the sewing table—for there was never a time when she wasn't working. Long after Tilly had gone to bed, she would hear the sewing machine, *trundle-trundle-trundle*, sounding through her dreams.

"Tilly."

"Oh, not yet—just another few minutes."

She had thought if she stayed as still as still, she might have been forgotten about, and gone to sleep here in the warmth, instead of having to uncramp herself all over again and go off into her icy bedroom.

"Tilly!" Now, there was a warning note in her mother's voice.

"All right."

She stood up. Saw the silk material, shining, creamy-white. Thought of Miss Kendall and her wedding and all the work it meant for her mother. Thought of Christmas.

Then she ran into her bedroom and turned on the washbasin faucet very, very quickly, before she had time to think about it, carrying a little of the warmth from the sitting room in with her.

When her mother came to say goodnight, Tilly asked, "Tomorrow after school, are we going to do a fitting?"

"No. That was the last for a while, I've just got to get on with it now. I shall be very busy, Tilly."

"Yes, I know. So please can I go down and see Mrs. McBride?"

Her mother hesitated for a moment.

"You and your Mrs. McBride."

"*Please.*"

She bent over, and tucked in Tilly's bed covers tightly.

"We'll see," she said, but in a voice that Tilly knew meant yes. "We'll have to see."

And then she went out, leaving the door just a little ajar as usual, for Tilly to see a line of light beneath it, from across the passage.

CHAPTER

2

The next school day was a very good one. There was a rehearsal for the Christmas play—Tilly had only a small part, as the innkeeper's wife, but she didn't mind: she loved the whole business of standing up and speaking her line and trying on her costume, and watching the others move around the stage, loved most of all the way that, even in school clothes, everybody seemed somehow different and a little strange, part of the other world of the far, hot country and the birth of a baby in a stable, the story-play-Bible world, not the ordinary one of here and everyday.

Then, after lunch and a lesson, they had made toffee in the kitchens for the rest of the afternoon, and a lot of the toffee sugared, but it didn't really matter. They were going to wrap it up in squares of cellophane, to be sold the next week at the Christmas bazaar, along with the lavender sachets and patchwork pincushions and the fluffy balls made out of bits of yarn wound around cardboard circles that they had been doing in needlework and handicraft all term.

But the pride of Tilly's life was the doll, Victoria Amelia, made and dressed by her own mother, with three changes of clothes, including lacy pantaloons and a tiny, fur-trimmed muff. Victoria Amelia was to be raffled. She had been held up at assembly to the whole school, and later put on display on a table in the front hall.

"Oh, Christmas, Christmas, Christmas!" sang Tilly all the way home at the end of the day.

And stopped yet again to admire the sweet jars and the chocolate figurines and the paper chains in the window of the corner shop.

"Oh, Christmas, Christmas, Christmas!"

Only the weather didn't feel very Christmassy: it was mild and muggy, and the air seemed to be heavy, to fill your lungs with water like bathroom steam, and there was a constant drizzling.

Christmas ought to be snow, snow and ice over the puddles and frost fingered into feathers on the window-panes, and sharp, bright cold. That was how it was in books, that was how they sang it every day in the carol practices.

"Deep and crisp and even..."

"In the bleak midwinter..."

That was how it surely ought to be.

"Be careful!" her mother called out as Tilly ran up the last flight of stairs. "Be careful!" And when Tilly opened the door, she saw why.

"Oh, it's *beautiful*!"

The silk for Miss Kendall's wedding dress was unrolled over the table, and cascading down in soft, shining folds

to the floor. The chairs had been pushed back and an old clean sheet spread over the carpet.

"You'll have to eat your snack in the kitchen, Tilly. I'm sorry, I can't risk anything being spilled in here. I'll have to clear it away soon, but I do want to finish the marking-out first."

"I don't mind."

Tilly didn't; she liked to stand in the tiny kitchen that was partitioned off from the living room, and so narrow there was no space for a table or chair, just a cupboard with a worktop, beside the sink. But between the two was a space into which she could still just squeeze, and then she could stand at the long window and look out, down into the yard below, or else over the rooftops and up at the sky. Even when it was dark she liked it, liked the moonlight and the stars, and the oblongs of light from the windows below.

But tonight, the drizzle and mist made them fuzzy, and bleared the windowpane.

Tilly took her plate of bread and jam and a slab of marble cake and ate quickly, and gulped down her milk, partly because she was very hungry and school lunch hours ago, but much more because she wanted to be off, down the stairs, to knock on the magic door.

"Can I go and see Mrs. McBride?"

"If you bolt your food like that you'll get indigestion."

"No I won't, I never do."

"Now, Miss Clever..."

"But can I *go*?"

Her mother looked at her, resting her hand lightly on the silk.

"I'd be out of your way, wouldn't I? You could get the pattern marked out."

"Yes." A shadow of something crossed her mother's face, worry or sadness? Tilly couldn't quite tell.

Then she said, "Poor Tilly. It's a bit miserable for you, I know, always having to make way for the sewing. If we just had a bit more space..." She didn't bother to finish, because they both knew there was no point. Larger apartments cost more to rent and they didn't have the money.

"If I could get a few more orders like this one... The trouble is, I've only got one pair of hands."

And then she held one of them out, and Tilly went to her, stepping very carefully around the silk, and her mother held her, and hugged her tight for a moment.

"But I don't want to neglect you."

"You don't, I'm all right."

"Are you? Did you have a good day at school?"

"Lovely, lovely," and she told, quickly, about the play rehearsal, and the toffee-making.

"And everybody thinks Victoria Amelia is beautiful, they all want to win her."

"Well, if it makes a pound or two more."

The Christmas bazaar was to raise money for refugees who had been forced to flee their own countries during the war, and still had no proper homes. They should do whatever they could, Tilly's mother had said.

"It might have been us, Tilly. We might have been refugees if men like your father hadn't died for their country."

"Yes, I know that," Tilly said, and pulled away. She didn't like it when her mother talked like that about her father, who had been killed in the war when Tilly was a baby; it gave her a strange, hot feeling in her stomach.

She felt confused, too. A part of her knew she should be proud of her father for dying and helping them to win the war—she had been told so enough times—but another part of her was angry with him for leaving them, so that her mother had to work and work and they still had so little money and had to live in a tiny attic apartment with horrible Mr. Simpkins for a landlord. Surely it was partly his own fault: lots of other soldiers and airmen had come back home, surely he could just have been more careful not to get killed?

But these were thoughts she could never speak.

"*Please* can I go to see Mrs. McBride? You said."

"I said 'we'll see'."

"Yes, well can we see *now?*"

Her mother laughed, and then turned back to the sewing table.

"Go on, but not for too long, and if it isn't convenient for her..."

"I'm to come straight back. I know, I know."

And Tilly escaped, to run lightly down the flights of

stairs and along the short passage to Mrs. McBride's apartment door.

It was always kept unlocked, and Tilly had agreed to a special way of knocking, so Mrs. McBride knew that it was her.

Rat-tat-tat-TAT—the first three taps the same, quite light, and the last much heavier—it was the V for Victory signal, Mrs. McBride had told her, they had played it every night on the wireless during the dark days of war.

Rat-tat-tat-TAT.

"Come in."

Whenever she opened Mrs. McBride's front door, Tilly always paused, to stand on the inner mat and close her eyes and sniff in the special and particular smell of the apartment. Most places had their own smell, their apartment smelled of material, and sewing-machine oil, the school hall smelled of polish and wood, her grandmother's house in Tenfield had smelled of coal smoke and smuts.

But Mrs. McBride's smelled of—*what* exactly? Ginger snaps, Tilly had finally decided. Ginger snaps and violet-scented soap, mixed with a trace of candle wax, a trace of silver polish, a trace of horsehair. Altogether, it was so powerful and pleasing that Tilly liked to fill her nostrils with it the second she arrived. *I'm here*, it made her feel, *I'm really here.*

Then she crossed the hall and pushed hard against the sitting room door, so that the draft-excluder sausage moved out of the way.

Mrs. McBride was lame. She could get up and walk slowly and stiffly across the room, using her two sticks. But most of the time she stayed in her chair, which was either turned to face the window, or the fire, with her feet up on a little round beaded stool.

The room was actually quite large, much larger than their own in the attic, but Mrs. McBride had so many things crowded into it, and particularly, some very big, dark pieces of furniture, that it seemed small, and cramped. Every corner had something in it, everywhere you looked were treasures. Tilly thought she could come and sit here every day for a year and still not see everything.

In the center of the room was the great round polished table, on which stood the blue and white patterned bowl, and which had six chairs around it. Apart from Mrs. McBride's armchair, there were two others, and a deep, soft sofa, covered in cushions, round and square, large and small, cushions, embroidered, tapestried, flowered, silk, satin, velvet, wool. There were other footstools, too, one embroidered with an elephant carrying a howdah on its back, and a brown leather hassock; a tall glass-fronted cabinet against one wall filled with china ornaments and

figurines, with flower-patterned plates, cups, bowls, dishes and jugs, and another against the opposite wall displaying glass, deep, deep blue and ruby red and crystal clear. There

were small tables draped with cloths that fell to the floor, on which stood pictures in silver frames—photographs of babies in christening robes and brides in huge, flower-brimmed hats, and soldiers with medals and mustaches and an old lady with stern eyes and her hair scraped tightly back. They were all of them from Mrs. McBride's family, her mother and grandmother, her sisters, her children, her grandchildren, and her animals too, several different small dogs, and a white pony harnessed to a governess cart.

The walls that did not have the cabinets or pictures of Scottish mountains and Italian lakes had shelves with more ornaments—a set of brass monkeys, a line of eight brass bells getting smaller in size as they went down, thimbles, and three tiny enamelled clocks. By the window there was a sewing box on a stand, lined with scarlet satin, and with all the needles, threads and buttons in special inlaid wooden trays. There were ivory lace-bobbins set out on a velvet cushion and a silver tea kettle and spirit lamp in the hearth and a fireplace screen painted over with shepherds and shepherdesses playing pipes in a woodland glade.

Beside Mrs. McBride's chair, next to the fire, were low cupboards, and inside the cupboards, more treasures, boxes filled with delights, beads and buttons, pictures sewn in silk, jewelry, old postcards, fans, a miniature set of farm-

yard animals, scraps of material from old wedding dresses
and christening robes, lace, and a piece of ribbon that had
come from an evening gown once worn by Queen Victoria.

Every time Tilly went there, Mrs. McBride would bring
out a different box, and with each box came a story, some
part of her past life.

Once, she had lived in a very large house, with a long
drive, and a morning room, a drawing room, her own
private sitting room, a breakfast room, and a parlor; there

had been maids and a butler and a cook and two gardeners and a nanny, and up to ten guests to stay from Friday to Monday.

But then her husband had died and her children had grown.

"And times changed, and I rattled around that house like a marble in a bread box," she had told Tilly. So she had moved to a much smaller house.

"But one of Hitler's bombs flattened *that* and so here I am."

The bomb had set fire to the smaller house, and a lot of things had been damaged beyond repair but there seemed to have been plenty left, and all of it now crammed tightly into this sitting room, one bedroom, and a kitchenette.

"Which is plenty of space for one old woman to take up in an overcrowded world."

Now Mrs. McBride turned as Tilly came in.

"Ah, there you are. If you would please to put a speck of coal on that fire, it would look more cheerful."

So Tilly did, and scraped away some of the cinders and ash beneath with the edge of the poker so that the flames came spurting through and the coal began to crackle.

"Well, that's much brighter and better on a dark wet night. Thank you, Matilda. And how are you?"

She was the only person in the world who ever called Tilly by her full and proper name and the only one, Tilly's mother said, who would be allowed by Tilly to get away with it, for she had been Tilly from the day of her birth, to everyone—not many people even knew she was called anything different.

"But Matilda is your christened name and a good one and I had a sister Matilda," Mrs. McBride had said one day, when Tilly had first begun to come down here.

"Where is she now?"

"She died of scarlet fever at the age of two. It was a terrible thing and a great sadness."

"Children did die of things then. More than nowadays," Tilly had said.

"But never let anyone tell you it didn't matter so much, because it did. Women bore eight and lost four but every one of them was loved and grieved over, every one of them was precious."

"Like your Matilda."

"Like her."

Now, Tilly settled on the hearthrug and began to fiddle with the fringe on a blanket that was spread over the armchair, as she told about the nativity play and the carol practices and the Christmas bazaar, and the wedding dress for Miss Kendall, and as Mrs. McBride listened, her plump fingers went stiffly in and out of her crochet and her rings glinted in the firelight and the oil painting of the cavalier in the lace collar looked down at them benignly from its place above the mantel.

Later, Mrs. McBride sent Tilly for the tin in the kitchen where the marshmallows were kept, and they toasted them on a brass fork over the fire. They dissolved, sweetly, softly, stickily, in their mouths, and Mrs. McBride drank her very small glass of Madeira wine to go with them: Tilly felt herself wrapped in quietness and comfort, and warmth and contentment.

They talked of a great many things, but most of all they talked about Christmas.

"In the window of the sweet shop there are figurines made out of chocolate, wrapped in shiny paper, and marzipan snowmen, and they've hung paper chains around the jars and the grocer has boxes of Christmas crackers."

"Ah," said Mrs. McBride, "but you should have seen the windows of the big department stores before the war." Her fingers worked in and out of the crochet, and the firelight gleamed on the gold frames of her spectacles.

"Tell me," Tilly said, and tucked her legs up more tightly beneath her. She liked to hear Mrs. McBride's

stories, about being a child in the country, and having grand parties in her married house. But most of all, she liked to hear about "before the war," which she always thought of as one long word. Her own mother talked about it sometimes, too. Beforethewar was a magical time, before the long dark days of bombs and blitz and blackout, of gas masks and air-raid sirens and queues and rationing and fathers gone to be soldiers.

"At Christmas, before the war," said Mrs. McBride, "when there was plenty of everything, the windows of all

the big stores had tableaux—scenes from stories—fairy tales and pantomime and nursery rhymes, with models of gnomes and woodcutters and gingerbread houses and Santa Claus's workshop and elfin glades and Cinderella and Puss in Boots and Aladdin's cave and the Snow Queen and—oh, anything you could dream of, and the models moved, wheels turned and axes chopped and snowflakes fell and stars twinkled, and everything was lit from within, they all shone out into the darkness of the street; and then inside the shops the goods were piled high, the crystallized fruits and jars of ginger, and brandied cherries and plum puddings and sugared almonds and marzipan pigs, and cakes with icing and scarlet ribbons. Oh, and the toys, such toys as *you* never saw, dolls dressed in satin ball gowns and Ascot hats, and baby dolls and sailor dolls and dolls' houses with real, working lights, and dolls' prams, and teddy bears as big as ponies and lions made of real fur and clockwork trains and forts full of soldiers and farmyards full of animals and model yachts to sail on the pond. There were pineapples and figs and melons and bananas from overseas, all heaped up, and sacks of nuts and wooden boxes of dates and raisins."

"Oh, I wish it was still Beforethewar," Tilly said,

looking into the fire, and trying to imagine the shops and the tableaux and the lights and the gold and silver.

"I daresay it will all come back one of these days, and more besides. But just now, Matilda, if you open my cupboard and take out the box that is tied with green string… I went looking in the bottom of the trunk this morning."

Mrs. McBride often "went looking in the bottom of the trunk," though it seemed to Tilly that actually the trunk didn't *have* a bottom, and must be the size of a cellar, too, so many things came out of it and there were always plenty more.

Now, she found the box, and gave it to Mrs. McBride, and then sat back on her heels, while the green string was carefully untied and rolled up into a ball and the box lid taken off.

Inside, she could see little mounds of yellowy-white tissue paper. Out came the first, then another, and another, and Mrs. McBride began carefully to unwrap each one. It took some time, and Tilly's eyes never left the box, and as she saw what was there, she felt all the old surprise and delight that came whenever Mrs. McBride found something in the cupboard, or a drawer, or opened a box or an envelope or a package; for every time it contained something beautiful or astonishing or amusing or rare or strange, and never like anything Tilly had seen before.

There had been a fan made of ostrich feathers, and a watchcase made of gold, a shawl embroidered all over with black jet beads, and a tumbling monkey and a jewel box of satin set inside a bird's egg, a wooden doll the size of a fingernail with a baby doll inside her the size of an orange seed.

"Go and switch off the big light, Matilda."

Tilly ran across the room and did so. "There now," Mrs. McBride said to her. And then Tilly turned, and looked around.

On the small table beside Mrs. McBride's chair, in the pool of light from the lamp, stood a slender column, with arms stretching out all around it like the graceful branches of a tree and the whole was made of clear crystal glass. But it might have been made of ice, Tilly thought, it glistened in just that way. Suspended from each of the branches by a silver thread as fine as a spider's skein, were angels, and the angels were made of crystal, too, with out-stretched wings and haloes, and robes that were swept up into an arc at the side, and the crystal was cut into patterns all over, like the goblets in Mrs. McBride's cabinet.

And the whole thing was turning very slowly, and as

it turned, the wings and haloes and outstretched robes of the angels caught the light and sparkled and glittered and the column gleamed and shone and music came tinkling from the revolving base—the music of the Rocking Carol.

Tilly crept slowly, softly, across the room, and stood close beside the table, holding her breath for fear that the whole thing might break in pieces or vanish somehow.

"Oh, beautiful," she whispered after a while. "Oh, beautiful," and together she and Mrs. McBride watched, as the shining crystal angels turned and turned to the gentle tune, and, looking at Mrs. McBride's face, Tilly saw that she was far away from this room and this time, was somewhere else, and with other people, remembering, remembering.

CHAPTER

3

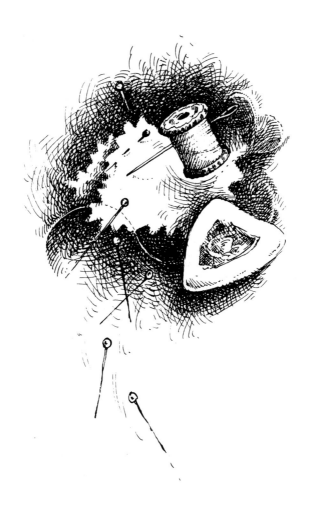

That night Tilly lay in bed, listening to the rain on the roof and, when she closed her eyes, seeing the crystal angels turning and sparkling. Her mother was still sewing, pinning up the wedding dress on the tailor's dummy. She would undress in the dark and slip into the other bed long after Tilly had gone to sleep.

But tonight, she had said that there was just one day more of work on it and then she would stop and begin to get ready for Christmas. She would come to the play and the bazaar and the carol service, and then it would be the last day of the school term, when Tilly would get out at lunchtime.

"And then, in the afternoon, we'll go shopping!"

"Can we have a tree this year, a real tree, with ornaments and silver chains, just a small one, in the corner?"

But the answer had been the usual one.

"We'll see."

There was already a fruitcake though, that had been made in October and stored away in a tin to mature. In a few days' time they would ice it.

They had spent last Christmas at Tadfield, with her mother's cousin Eleanor Flint. She had made Tilly call her Aunt Flint. It hadn't been a very happy time. Tilly's mother and Aunt Flint did not get on, and the house had been cold and polished and tidy, and there had been no decorations apart from a single line of Christmas cards on the mantelpiece.

The dressmaking business had been very slack all that year. There had been lots of the hated renovations and alterations which were more trouble than they were worth, and paid very little; Tilly's presents had been a new pair of woolen gloves, and a pencil case, and a red book of stories that had belonged to Aunt Flint when she was a girl and Aunt Flint had questioned her the whole time about what she did at school, and complained that she had "grown so" and banged doors.

"Next year, we'll stay at home. Just the two of us," Tilly's mother had said, tightening her lips, but even that, Tilly thought guiltily, did not sound very exciting.

Mrs. McBride was going to spend two days with friends; she was to be fetched by car. Tilly tried not to think of that, she did not want the lamp not to be shining through the gap in the curtains and the apartment to be empty and closed-up when she went past.

"And we must take down a Christmas dinner for Miss Brookes," her mother had said the previous day. "She has no one at all in the world, poor soul. I'd ask her up here to share it with us, but she'd never manage the stairs."

*

Now, lying in bed, Tilly prayed that she wouldn't have to take the dinner down, as she sometimes had to take odd bits of shopping. She was afraid of Miss Brookes. Her apartment had a bead curtain in the kitchen doorway that clacked softly, and it smelled sour, and Miss Brookes talked to herself, had dirty fingernails and gypsy earrings and wild eyes and a shrieky parrot in a cage that was hardly ever cleaned out.

Her mother said she was just very lonely and neglected and rather forgetful. But Tilly always tried to get away as quickly as she could and not let Miss Brookes catch her and hold her by the arm with her hands that gripped as tight as claws.

To keep herself from thinking about it, Tilly turned over on her other side and made the picture of the crystal angels come before her eyes, and tried to remember all the things Mrs. McBride had said used to be in the shops Beforethewar. She wanted to dream about all of that, not about Miss Brookes and the terrible parrot.

The play was a great success, and at the bazaar, a girl in Tilly's class called Louisa Truman won the doll, Victoria Amelia. She was so overcome with surprise and pleasure that she grabbed Tilly around the waist and danced her all the way down the school hall, and when they got back up to the top again, out of breath, she said:

"And I want you to come to my Boxing Day party. I've told my mother and you're to ask yours. It's going to be really good, with an entertainer and an ice cream cake but you'll have to wear pumps and a party dress. Have you got a party dress?"

Tilly stood up very straight. "Yes, of course."

"That's all right then."

Though Tilly saw the look of anxiety that crossed her mother's face when she told her.

"Your party dress is from two years ago. It's much too small and I haven't time to make you another one and you don't have any pumps—would slippers do? And they live at The Uplands don't they, one of those big houses on the cliff road beyond Miss Kendall's, and there wouldn't be any buses on Boxing Day, we'd have to walk, and..." Her voice trailed off, but then she smiled at Tilly.

"But there, I expect we can manage somehow. If you really do want to go. I didn't know Louisa Truman was much of a friend of yours."

"Yes, she is," said Tilly quickly.

It was a lie though. She hardly knew Louisa Truman, who had only been at the school for two years, and did not really like her. She had felt a great thud of disappointment in her stomach when her name had been read out as the winner of Victoria Amelia.

The worst had been the day Louisa had called Tilly "a free place child," and lots of the class had turned around to stare.

"What is a free place child?" Tilly had demanded, bursting into the apartment that afternoon. "Am I one?"

Her mother had laid down her scissors, looking upset.

"Yes," she had said quietly. "Yes, you are. There are a few free places at your school for girls who deserve to

have a good education but whose families can't afford the school fees."

"Because their fathers were killed in the war."

"Or sometimes for other reasons. It isn't anything to be ashamed of, Tilly. But I'd like to know how it got out and who it was who told you."

But Tilly had refused to say.

Now though, the thought of the Boxing Day party made her push it all down to the bottom of her mind; it shone out like a beacon. She would wear a party dress somehow, she knew her mother would manage something, and perhaps even buy her some pumps out of Miss Kendall's money, for surely she would understand that to go in furry slippers would be awful.

On the day of the carol service, Tilly's mother had a cough at breakfast that even three cups of hot tea did not soothe. She sat at the back of the church, which was very cold indeed, and Tilly could see her coughing into her handkerchief so as not to make any disturbance. On the way home, her face was flushed and her eyes oddly bright.

"I'm afraid I'm coming down with a cold, Tilly."

"Will you be better tomorrow?"

"Oh, yes, I expect so. But I think it would be a good

idea if I went to bed early tonight, and had a hot drink and an aspirin. Will you be all right?"

"Of course I will."

Tilly felt important, helping her mother to bed, as if she were grown-up and in charge of things now, though inside she felt a bit uncertain. She could not remember her mother being ill like this ever before.

All that night she coughed, and the next morning she was obviously worse. When she got out of bed to go to the bathroom, she had to clutch hold of the bedhead.

"I don't think I can stand up, Tilly. I think it must be influenza—I do feel very poorly."

"What shall I do?" Tilly asked anxiously. "Should I go and tell Mrs. McBride? Shall I go to the telephone box and ring for the doctor?"

"Oh, no, no, I'll be fine. I'll just go back to sleep. I'm sure that will get me better. But you'll have to make your own breakfast and get yourself ready for school. Can you manage? And I'm afraid we won't be able to go shopping this afternoon, as I promised."

"Will you be better tomorrow?"

"Oh yes, of course."

But Tilly didn't think she sounded very certain.

*

The last morning of the term, and all the excitement of breaking up for Christmas lost some of its edge, as Tilly worried about her mother and wondered what would happen, what she should do. There wasn't much time left to get ready, and what if… She knew she ought to think just of her mother getting well, only she felt she could not bear it if, when this year Christmas had promised to be special, suddenly there was no Christmas for them at all.

She ran all the way home from the bus, through the early dark and drizzle, not even stopping to look in the window of the corner sweet shop.

Her mother seemed very ill indeed.

"Tilly, I think perhaps you *had* better ring the doctor. There's some change for the telephone in my purse. And would you go to the grocer's, we need bread and cheese and some eggs, and get a bottle of lemon barley water. I'm so thirsty."

All the time she was talking, she coughed, and her face looked shiny and damp, and her eyes seemed to have sunken into her head and gone darker.

Tilly made herself a jam sandwich with the last of the bread, and went out, eating it from her hand.

She didn't care about Christmas now, she had forgotten it, because she was frightened. Her mother had looked so ill, and her father was already dead, so what if... She stood stock-still in the roadway.

If her mother died, she would have no one at all, except Aunt Flint, in the cold, tidy house in Tadfield.

She began to run, clutching the coins in her hand tightly. By the time she reached the telephone kiosk, she was so out of breath she had to wait before she could speak to the person who answered at Dr. Craddock's.

"Hmm," he said, as he sat beside her mother late that afternoon, his hand on the pulse at her wrist. She was lying still now, but when Tilly had got back she had been restlessly tossing, throwing off the bed covers and muttering to herself. Once, she had half sat up and cried out and Tilly had gone in, but it was as though her mother could not see her, she stared through her somehow, before falling back on her pillows.

"Your mother is really quite ill, Tilly. I don't like the sound of her chest and she has a very high fever—she could come down with pneumonia."

Dr. Craddock looked at her intently. Tilly had known him ever since she could remember, he had treated her mumps and measles and tonsillitis and put stitches in her lip when she had fallen onto a sharp rock.

Now she saw how serious his face was and a cold feeling ran down her spine. Then he stood and beckoned her into the sitting room.

"We'll leave her to sleep."

He sat down on the arm of a chair.

"She's going to die, isn't she?" The inside of Tilly's mouth was dry, and her tongue seemed oddly big, as she spoke the words.

"Oh no, no, she won't die. But she *is* very ill and I'm concerned about you here alone—is there no one who could come and stay?"

"No, we don't have anybody."

Tilly pushed the thought of Aunt Flint away. "But I can look after her, if you tell me what I have to do."

"I was really thinking of sending her to the hospital."

"*No*, oh, please—she'd hate that, she *can't* be in the hospital for Christmas. And besides, if she did..."

"What would happen to you?"

"I can give her medicine and get drinks, I can help her wash. I can light the gas and make eggs on toast and come to the telephone if she gets worse—and there are people in the apartments downstairs."

"Well—that's true I suppose..." He waited a moment, then stood up.

"And I'll come in each day. I'll leave two bottles of medicine now, and try to make sure she has plenty to drink but otherwise, let her sleep. And if you're at all worried about anything, ring my home—have you enough coins for the telephone?"

When he had gone, Tilly went into the kitchen and stood in the window space, looking down. It was dark now, and still raining, the sound of it running down the gutters was comforting, it made her feel less alone.

But after a time, she felt afraid about things again. Her mother was sleeping. Tilly put a jug of barley water and a glass on the table beside her, and a note in case she awoke, and leaving the door unlocked, slipped downstairs.

"I mustn't stay for long," she said, standing on the hearthrug beside Mrs. McBride's chair.

And then she poured out everything, about her mother's illness that the doctor feared might turn to pneumonia, and what else that he had said, and old Mrs. McBride's hands lay still on her crochet, as she listened.

"And she won't be able to go out, and in three days it will be Christmas—only it won't, we shan't *have* a Christmas, shall we, not at all? Oh, it isn't fair, it isn't *fair*."

Tilly cried then, not only tears of worry and fear, but of anger, too.

Mrs. McBride waited until she had quieted down.

"Well now, you'll feel much better after that. Poor Matilda, and your poor mother, too—not much of a Christmas for her, either."

"No," said Tilly, blowing her nose.

"When you've finished, go into my kitchen and look in the cupboard against the wall, to the right. You'll see a bottle of syrup."

When Tilly brought it, she said, "That mixture has cured a good many coughs and nasty chests, it will do your mother a power of good. Now—under a cloth in the larder is half an apple pie. I ate mine for lunch and your mother won't be feeling like any, but I daresay you will— put a drop of cream on it. And the third thing is over there, on the sideboard. I've been to the bottom of the old trunk again today."

It was another of Mrs. McBride's brown cardboard boxes.

"Now those," she said, "we had on the tree at my married home, every single year, and when I was a child before that. The rest were lost when the bomb fell—those are the last few left."

Carefully, one by one, Tilly took out seven Christmas tree ornaments. They felt so light and so fine in her hand,

she was afraid they might break just by being touched. There were two golden and two silver spheres, on fine thread; a glistening holly-tree cone with red berries fashioned out of the glass; there was a bird with a long tail feather, peacock green and blue, and an iridescent sheen over its body that gleamed in the light, and a pointed glass star with fine silver brushwork on the tips.

"You may not be having a tree," said Mrs. McBride, "but you could surely find some place to hang them—or just set them on the windowsill to catch the light."

"Thank you," Tilly said. "Oh, they're lovely and I will be very, very careful with them."

Upstairs, she ate the apple pie with some cheese, and a piece of chocolate she found at the back of a drawer, and her mother had a drink, and a spoonful of Mrs. McBride's syrup, as well as the doctor's medicine. The syrup looked horrible, dark treacly brown and sticky and her mother said it was bitter, and puckered up her mouth in disgust at it. But before long she slept again more peacefully, though she still looked very pale, and thinner, suddenly, thinner and older.

"Tilly, are you all right, my love? What's happening about everything? Can you manage?"

But she did not wait for any proper answer, or seem

to have the strength to go on worrying, just turned her head on the pillow, and closed her eyes.

Tilly put on the gas fire and sat beside it with a book in her lap. But she couldn't properly take in what she was reading and in the end she gave up and just sat, wondering. Tomorrow she thought she could go out to the shops herself to buy whatever they needed, the Christmas chicken and vegetables, and if her mother told her how, carefully, surely she would be able to cook them, and she could get fruit and perhaps some sweets. The doctor would come again, too, and then surely her mother would begin to get better? It would be all right just as long as she did not have to go into the hospital, and Tilly be sent to Aunt Flint.

But oh, it did not seem like Christmas, Tilly thought, and wished again that there might be cold and ice and snow. At least then it would look right. She went to the window again and looked out. "At least it would *feel* more like Christmas."

But there was still only the rain, more and more of it, and the darkness and the wind, so that in the end, Tilly drew the curtains tightly, and went to bed, feeling lonelier than she had ever felt in her life.

As she crossed the room, she passed close to Miss

Kendall's wedding dress, cut out and tacked and pinned up on the dummy, with the cascade of silk material that would form the train, spreading out behind. Tilly touched it lightly. It felt cold, and yet warm, too, and slippery-smooth, yet with a slight roughness that caught against the pads of her fingers.

When it was finished, it would have embroidery and beading and a scalloped hem, and fine seaming at the neck and cuffs and on the bodice, and Miss Kendall would look like a bride in a picture.

Now, on the stand, the half-made dress gleamed pale and ghost-like and all at once, Tilly wished it were not there, like some silent, dead companion, and she went quickly away into the bedroom, and closed the door.

CHAPTER

4

She woke with a start, and sat up. Her mother was coughing again, but when Tilly called to her softly, she did not reply. It must have been the rain that had awakened her, that and the wind beating at the windows. But it seemed to her that she had heard another sound, too, a creak or a crack. Now though, there was nothing and after a while, she lay down again, and burrowed deep under the bedclothes, not so much for warmth as for comfort, the feeling of loneliness black and gnawing like hunger inside her.

When she slept again, dreams came crowding in on her, confused and peculiar and frightening, it was as though she knew she was asleep and tried to bring herself awake, but could not.

The next morning was dark, but at last, Tilly noticed, the rain had stopped. She would get up and make her mother a cup of tea. Perhaps she would be better today. Though in her heart, Tilly knew that even if she were, better would still not mean well enough for them to have a proper Christmas.

Only it did not seem to matter now, her mother's illness, coming so suddenly, had frightened Tilly, and made her feel very much alone; all she wanted was for it to be over, and for her mother to be well.

She got out of bed, and went across the passage, and

opened the sitting room door, and then she gave a cry, except that the cry stuck in her throat and did not come out. She simply stood, in horror, silent and staring, staring.

There had been a long crack across the ceiling of the living room ever since Tilly could remember—a friendly sort of crack, she had somehow thought of it. But now it was not friendly at all. It was much wider, ugly and jagged and some of the plaster around it had broken away and fallen. And through the crack water, dirty water, was dripping steadily—it looked as if it had been dripping through all night, onto the tailor's dummy and Miss Kendall's white silk wedding dress and the train, and the roll of material spread out on the floor behind it. The wedding dress was quite wet and stained with dark brown, muddy stains. There was a puddle on the train, and the carpet all around was wet, too, and droppings of plaster and dirt lay on it and on the table.

Tilly knew, even in the midst of her shock and confusion and muddle, that she ought to put something under the hole to catch any more rain that might at any moment begin to fall in again, and she went to the kitchen and got a bowl, and the bucket from under the sink. But she had no idea how to begin to clear up the mess. Only whatever happened, her mother must not find out, not

yet, while she was still so ill; somehow, Tilly knew she must keep it from her. It was not the ceiling that mattered, or even the carpet and the chair, it was the fact that Miss Kendall's wedding dress had been completely ruined, and Tilly had heard her mother say that the silk alone had cost forty pounds. And where would another forty pounds come from?

Then she realized, standing in the sitting room, amongst the fallen plaster and water and ruined dress, that she did not know what else to do, she could not manage alone now. Her mother being ill and Christmas in two days' time had been bad enough, but this was different.

Perhaps it was *her* fault that the plaster had fallen in, perhaps she should have noticed that something was wrong last night, a wider crack or a damp patch.

She felt muddled and troubled and frightened, but beneath all of that, which was churning up her stomach like a stormy sea, she felt oddly calm, and sure, suddenly, about what she must do first and for the best.

She went quietly into the bedroom and dressed, and then stuffed her pillow down inside her bed and pulled the covers right up. In the gray light of early morning, it might look to her mother as if she was still in bed, humped up asleep.

"Please don't let her find it," she said, an urgent, whispered-aloud prayer. "Please let her stay asleep."

And then she went, pulling on her coat and boots in the hallway, and running down all the flights of stairs in the dark, in case the click of the light switch should wake her mother. At the end of the corridor to Mrs. McBride's, she hesitated. But no, Mrs. McBride could not climb up the stairs or go out with her for help, she was an old lady, she was for visiting and talking to, telling things, and being with companionably—but for now, this was different.

The streets were quiet, curtains still drawn at windows. No one was around. It had not begun to rain again, but as the gray dawn seeped up over the sea, Tilly saw that the sky was full of great-bellied, scudding clouds, and when she turned onto the esplanade, the sea was white-flecked and dirty-looking, heaving about within itself.

She wished she had a bicycle, it seemed further than she had remembered, and although she ran when she could, it soon gave her a stitch in her side and she was forced to slow down to a walk again.

For a short way up the last hill towards Cliff House, a small brown dog appeared out of some bushes, and ran alongside her, and Tilly felt cheered by it and wished it

would keep her company all the way. But when she reached the top of the sea front road, and turned left, she saw it scampering back, answering a distant whistle.

She had never been as far as this by herself—perhaps, if circumstances had been different, she might have enjoyed it, smelling the salt on the air and feeling independent, passing the closed-up hotels and dreaming of summer, imagining. Only now she was hardly aware of her surroundings, she was simply kept going by the urgency of where she had to go, and why.

Then, she reached the great, double-fronted house, and saw a light on, and felt her heart pounding, as she scrunched and scurried up the gravel drive to the steps, and the front door.

A man opened it, a small, bald man with a mustache. He was wearing a red bathrobe.

"Well, bless me," he said, looking Tilly closely up and down. "Who in heaven's name are you?"

"I'm Tilly," she said, and then faltered, and began again.

"My name is Matilda Cumberland and please may I see Miss Kendall... it's... it's very, very important."

And then, without any warning to herself at all, she burst into tears.

Behind the man, as he brought her inside, she heard someone else, saw a woman, though not Miss Kendall.

"Good gracious, Gerald. I think it's the dressmaker's child!"

When they had been to this house before, for Miss Kendall to choose patterns and be measured, Miss Kendall's mother had been kind enough to Tilly but distant—her smile had not been the sort of smile that meant warmth and friendship, just politeness. Tilly thought they were rich and grand and snobbish, and she had not liked the way Mrs. Kendall had called her "the dressmaker's child" just now.

But whatever they thought of her, they showed only concern and helpfulness. She was taken not into the little back parlor but the dining room, where there was a fire and silver candlesticks and a Christmas tree in the window, and breakfast was set out, and they made her have hot milk with honey stirred into it and porridge with cream, and Miss Kendall was fetched down, and sat beside her, and her hair floated loose onto her shoulders, and she looked younger and somehow softer, Tilly thought. Her brother was there too, Mr. Alec Kendall, and he waved a slice of toast at Tilly and winked, and spoke with his mouth full.

But it was hard to smile or swallow the food. She was so afraid, full of the enormity of what had happened, and the awfulness of what she had to tell them. Yet when she did, pouring it out in a great rush, somehow it was all right, in spite of the way they all sat around her and stared at her in silence as she spoke.

"And you say your mother hadn't woken up when you came out, she knows nothing of this?" asked Mr. Kendall.

"No, but she might have woken up now, I'll have to go back." She turned to Miss Kendall. "You see, the dress is completely spoiled, that's what I had to come and tell you, it's wet and covered with plaster and dirt, I don't think any of the material could be saved, and Mother said

it cost forty pounds—only she doesn't have forty pounds, she couldn't buy any more, and the money she was earning for making it was going to pay the bills and—and it was for a proper Christmas, too."

She tried to swallow hard, and she dug her fingers into the palms of her hands but it was no use at all, she couldn't stop herself from crying all over again.

After that, a great many things happened, a tumble of things one after another, and in the end, Tilly just gave up and let them, because the Kendalls seemed to know best and to want to take charge and sort everything out.

Telephone calls were made, and Miss Kendall went

away to get dressed, and her brother persuaded Tilly to eat a peach, and the juice ran down her chin, and he threw her his napkin to mop it up, and winked at her again. She had only tasted a peach once in her life before, and that had been in the summer, and ever after that day, Tilly was to think of rich people as the ones who had peaches to eat in December.

And then the car was brought around, and on the way home they stopped at a builder's yard, where Mr. Kendall had a talk with a man about the ceiling, and then they were swishing up through the puddles to the front of the apartment building.

"I'll go first," Tilly said, scrambling out. She had liked the car; it had smelled of leather and oil and the seats were squashy and cool against the backs of her legs.

"I'll go first in case..." and Miss Kendall nodded and touched her shoulder reassuringly, and Tilly saw her glance at her father, as they climbed all the stairs to the attic.

As soon as they neared the last flight, Tilly heard her mother coughing—coughing and crying.

She was sitting on the arm of the chair beside the table in her nightgown, amongst the rubble and the plaster, and the rain dripping into the bowl and bucket, and the spoiled wedding dress. For a moment, seeing Tilly, she looked frightened, and her face was as pale as the ghostly silk, but then she reached out and held onto Tilly, and could do nothing else but cry, and Tilly knelt beside her, stroking her arm and her hand. "It's all right," she said. "It's going to be all right now," and she had a strange sensation of having changed places with her mother, and done all her growing up overnight, so that she was in charge and knew what to do, and her mother was the helpless child.

The rest of the day was a confusion of comings and goings, the apartment had never been so full of so many people. The doctor came, and a builder called Mr. Rourke, and then Mr. Simpkins, their landlord, and he seemed a very different man, talking respectfully to Mr. and Miss Kendall, from the way he was with Tilly's mother. A grocer's delivery van and a butcher's boy arrived with parcels of food, and later, a nurse that Miss Kendall and the doctor had arranged for appeared, to give Tilly's mother a wash, and change her sheets, take her temperature and settle her down again on plumped-up pillows. She was actually a little better, the doctor said. While she had slept, her body had fought a battle against the infection and had begun to win; with care she would not get pneumonia now. But she was still quite ill, and

must be properly looked after for at least a week.

"In the hospital?" Tilly asked anxiously.

"Well…" he hesitated, "she doesn't really need that now, but…"

"Certainly she doesn't," Miss Kendall said, "she must come to Cliff House. There are spare rooms, and the nurse can come in every day. They can spend Christmas with us."

For a moment, it seemed to Tilly that there was nothing she could do, it had all been taken out of their hands and settled, and perhaps it would be a good thing, and her mother would have a chance to get well and be properly looked after, and the Kendalls had such a beautiful Christmas tree—and peaches…

She sat on the sofa. Mr. Kendall had gone downstairs with Mr. Simpkins, and the builder was starting to clear up all the plaster rubble into a sack. He whistled as he did it. Tilly liked him.

"What will happen to the roof?" she asked.

"Oh, we'll patch it up and keep the old rain out for now. But next week, I'll be back to fix it good and proper." He made it sound as if it were nothing to him, just nothing at all, when Tilly had wondered this morning if the whole house would collapse, and they would have to find another apartment.

"Made a real old mess, didn't it? But things generally look worse than they are."

It was looking better already, he was right. The hole didn't seem nearly so gaping or the pile of rubble so huge.

"Will it cost a lot of money to mend?"

"Cost your old landlord a bob or two, but that's not your worry, is it?"

So Mr. Kendall really had dealt with Mr. Simpkins. Everything seemed to be running away like an express train. She ought to be glad, and grateful, and she *was,* she was ... only...

"Tilly—Tilly, where are you?"

Her mother was propped up on two pillows, her hair brushed back from her face, which had just a little bit of color in it. The nurse had set out her medicines, and a jug of barley water covered with a cloth, and a sponge in a bowl, neatly on the bedside table. She would be back that evening, she had said. Tilly sat on the edge of the bed.

"Do you feel better?"

"Yes, weak, but somehow having the nurse—and knowing everything is being taken care of and that you're all right..."

"Yes."

"They've been very, very kind."

"Yes."

"I was so afraid when I realized you'd gone, and by yourself all that way—but you did the right thing, Tilly."

"Yes."

They fell silent, looking at one another. Then Tilly said very quietly, "Only I don't think I want to go there for Christmas."

"But Tilly—oh, love, no more do I—only we don't have anything and I couldn't go shopping—I expect it would be quite grand there—but you would have such a dull time here with me—I did get you one present but I haven't even had a chance to wrap it and—"

"But I just want to be us," Tilly interrupted, "at home. It doesn't matter about that. I don't want to go to the Kendalls, it wouldn't feel right."

"No."

There was the sound of the door then, and Miss Kendall's voice calling.

"I'll go." Tilly slid quickly off the bed. "I'll tell her."

If Miss Kendall was puzzled or offended, she did not show it, just said she understood, and made Tilly promise that she would telephone them for anything that might be needed, and said her mother was not to worry about the hole in the ceiling or the spoiled dress, but only about getting herself completely better.

"And the nurse will come in, of course, that's all taken care of," which Tilly knew meant "paid for." Only her mother said that one day she meant to pay the Kendalls back for that, because although they had been very generous and kind, it was better "not to be beholden."

At the end of the afternoon, when everyone had left, there was a bump at the door, and when Tilly opened it, Mr. Alec Kendall was there, grinning at her over the top of a huge hamper.

"Hang on," he said, setting it down on the table. "Back in a jiff."

When he appeared again, he was carrying a Christmas tree, set in a large pot.

"All in order. Good show," and he winked at her, and was gone.

Tilly walked around the tree, touching the branches here and there. It was quite bare and smelled freshly green and pungent, as though it were still growing outside. She could have Mrs. McBride's ornaments on it, and perhaps some bits of ribbon from her mother's scrap box, tied in bows.

Mrs. McBride—oh, she must see her, she must tell her everything … only then she remembered that Mrs. McBride would have gone away already, the apartment would be dark.

"Christmas," she said aloud to the tree, "Christmas, Christmas, Christmas."

But the room did not look like a Christmas room, and just for a moment, she wished she could change her mind and be going to Cliff House, where everything would be grand and bright and full of glitter and excitement.

Only she knew that it would not do, just as it would not do to go to Louisa Truman's Boxing Day party, where she would have felt out of place as well, and Louisa's

sudden rush of friendliness towards her after winning the doll would have quite faded.

But one day, Tilly thought, standing in the window space and looking out, one day.

All the same, it was a good Christmas, very, very good, even if everything was upside-down and unexpected. The hamper had been full of treats, things they would never have had, crystallized fruits and chocolates and pears in brandy, and a pineapple and six peaches, and mince pies and marzipan animals, a ham and a tongue and a cold roast chicken, and even a little flat packet of smoked salmon, which her mother said she had not seen since long

Beforethewar, and a bottle of sherry, and a tin of iced cookies. There were some crackers, too, and some scented soaps and a decorated candle in a little china holder.

And at the bottom, in an envelope, forty pounds, in notes, to buy a new roll of wedding dress silk.

Late on Christmas Eve, they had a picnic in the bedroom, and afterwards, for half an hour, Tilly's mother got up and sat in the armchair and enjoyed the tree and Mrs. McBride's ornaments, and Tilly lit the Christmas candle, and set it in the window.

As her mother was settling down to sleep, she said, "Oh, Tilly, I quite forgot—a parcel was left for you on the doormat. Miss Kendall found it."

Tilly picked up a familiar small cardboard box, tied with green string. It had an envelope slipped under it.

Dear Matilda,

My nephew will deliver this to you as we leave. I wish you both a very happy Christmas, and you are please to open this on Christmas Eve, not wait until the morning. It is for you to enjoy this year and then to keep and bring out every Christmas to come, until you are an old, old, gray-haired lady like your friend,

Christobel McBride

Tilly turned to her mother to read the letter out loud, but she saw that she was already asleep, settled on the pillow with her arm curved up behind her head. Tilly took the box and tiptoed out.

In the living room, she turned off the main light, and sitting beside the window close to the Christmas candle, she lifted out the crystal tree, with all its angels, and set it on the sill, and wound it up with the tiny golden key in the base. The window was slightly open, and a faint breeze blew in, flickering the flame of the candle, and as the angels went around, they swung a little and glinted as they caught the light and touched against each other, to make a faint ringing sound. And looking up, out of the window, Tilly saw that the rain had stopped and the clouds had parted, and there were stars pricked out in the clear sky, stars and a sliver of silver moon.

"Oh, beautiful," she whispered, "oh, beautiful," and sat, watching the crystal angels in the candlelight, until she fell into a half-sleep, half-waking trance, her head on her arm.

Every year, every single Christmas, she would watch the angels turning and hear their music, here in this room and then in other rooms she had not yet seen, on and on into the far future, until she was "an old, old, gray-haired lady."

It seemed as if she could see into that future, see the

pictures of it, like the tableaux in the lighted shop windows of the past. The angels were a symbol to her of happiness to come, as they had played their part in so many happy Christmases before.

One day, Tilly thought, one day...

And for a while, she did fall asleep, very lightly, as she sat there.

And was awakened by the first of the midnight bells of Christmas, ringing out across the town.